*American Frontier #3*

# DAVY CROCKETT AND THE PIRATES AT CAVE-IN ROCK

Based on the Walt Disney Television Show

Written by A. L. Singer
Cover Illustrated by Mike Wepplo
Illustrated by Charlie Shaw

DISNEP PRESS
NEW YORK

FIRST EDITION

1   3   5   7   9   10   8   6   4   2

Library of Congress Catalog Card Number: 91-71355
ISBN 1-56282-003-6/1-56282-002-8 (lib. bdg.)

Consultant: Judith A. Brundin, Supervisory Education Specialist
National Museum of the American Indian
Smithsonian Institution, New York

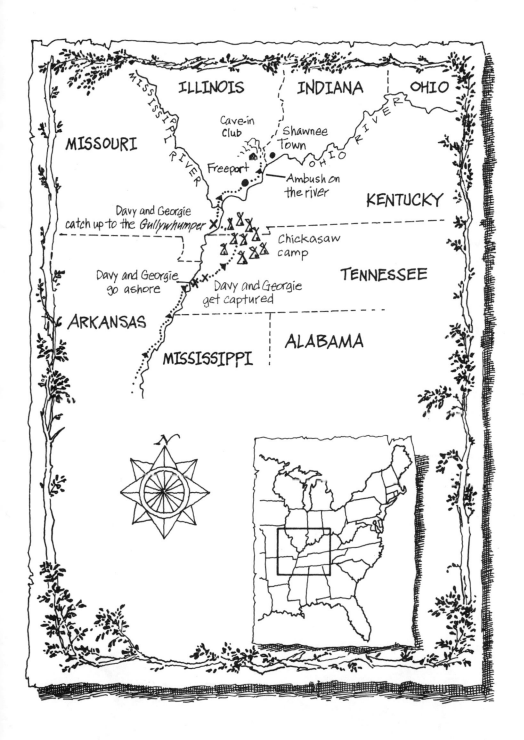

## CHAPTER 1

"Pole!" shouted big Mike Fink to his crew, from the back of his keelboat, the *Gullywhumper*.

His crewmen lifted their wooden poles out of the water. "Yahh!" they grunted as they plunged the poles back in. When they felt the poles hit the river bottom, they pushed hard against it.

The flat-bottomed boat surged forward, as Mike steered it through the water.

*Swisshh!* went the Mississippi River.

"Pole!"

"Yahh!"

*Swisshh!*

Davy Crockett wiped the sweat off his brow. He and his friend Georgie Russel had joined Big Mike's crew for this trip upriver. Now, Davy and Georgie were just about two of the strongest men in the whole country, but they were getting tired. It had been "Pole," "Yahh," and *swish* all the way up the long, long river.

Davy Crockett was not only one of the strongest men in the country but also one of the most famous men in the early 1800s. Everyone knew at least one good Davy Crockett story.

Some of the stories were true. And some were not so true, but everyone loved telling tall tales about Davy Crockett—even Davy!

There was the story about the time that Davy caught a bear when he was only three years old. Or the time that he convinced a raccoon to come out of a tree and jump into his supper pot just by grinning at it.

Then there was the adventure that led Davy and Georgie to be here, on Mike Fink's boat. It seems Davy and Georgie needed to take a pile of furs all the way down the Ohio River to Natchez, Mississippi. Well, Georgie got to bragging, and before he knew it he had challenged Mike Fink's crew to a keelboat race that would go down the Ohio and the Mississippi rivers, south past Natchez and all the way to New Orleans, Louisiana. Problem was, Davy and Georgie didn't know anything about keelboats, and Mike Fink wasn't called the King of the River for nothing!

But Davy wasn't one to back down from a challenge, and he led his boat—once he found one, that is—to victory. Not only that, but during the race, Davy even saved tough old Mike Fink's life. It happened in Shawneetown, Illinois, on the Ohio River, when the *Gullywhumper* was attacked by some Indians.

Now, Mike may have been a rough, ornery guy, but he wasn't a sore loser. He did just what he had agreed to do if he lost—he ate his big green felt hat, red feather and all! And, after that, Mike became good friends with Davy and Georgie. He even invited them to get back home by helping the *Gullywhumper* crew take a shipment of molasses upriver, which is just what they were doing.

But friend or not, Mike was a hard captain to please!

"Pole!" he shouted again. "Put your backs into it! What do you think this is, a free trip?"

"Why, you ungrateful polecat!" Georgie yelled. "We shoved and dragged this old tub of yours all the way up from New Orleans!"

Mike grinned. "I got to admit, for a couple of backwoods bear hunters, you ain't done bad."

"Those are mighty kind words coming from you, Mike," Davy said. He searched the riverbank. There were trees and fields but no sign of human beings. Even so, Davy knew this was the right spot. To the east was Tennessee and a few miles north Mike would leave the Mississippi to follow the Ohio River. "You can put us ashore any place along here," he said. Mike moved the tiller, and the *Gullywhumper* veered to the right. "I can't see why you bristle-headed varmints can't land at a settlement like civilized passengers."

"How do you like that?" Georgie said with a laugh.

"He works the tar out of us, and then he calls us *passengers*!"

Davy was still squinting at something on the riverbank. "Yep," he said, "this'll be the quickest way to get home."

"Home?" Mike replied. "From here? Seems like a mighty long walk to me."

"Who's walking?" Georgie said. "We're going to get some horses and sit down for a change."

"Now, where are you going to find horses in a lonesome place like this?" Mike asked.

"The Chickasaw tribe," Davy answered. "This is their country, and they're real friendly. I'm sure they'll have some horses to sell."

The *Gullywhumper* stopped by the riverbank. Davy and Georgie shook hands with Mike. "Been a real pleasure knowing you," Davy said.

"I ain't likely to forget you two, neither," Mike said with a smile.

Davy and Georgie climbed off the *Gullywhumper* and onto the riverbank. Davy liked the feeling of solid earth under his feet. It had been a long boat ride.

"Hey!" Mike called out, pointing to a knee-high burlap bag by the cabin. "What about that heavy sack you brought in from New Orleans? You acted like it was so goldarn important you couldn't even tell us what was in it. Now you're plumb leaving it like a sack of garbage."

"Oh, that's yours," Georgie told him.

"Mine?" Mike asked.

Davy grinned. "Just a little something to remember us by."

"Open it up," Georgie said.

Mike reached in and pulled out a small steel cannon. It would have been too heavy for most people to lift. But not for Big Mike. He held it up high with admiration. "Well, ain't she a pretty little popgun!"

As the entire crew gathered around, Mike noticed a message engraved on the cannon. He read it aloud:

" 'To Mike Fink, King of the River, from his admirers, Davy Crockett and G. E. Russel.' "

"Well, now that we're leaving, we figured you needed something to protect you in case of any more attacks upriver," Georgie said.

"After your help on the way down, I don't reckon anyone'll be too eager to attack the *Gullywhumper* again," Mike replied, "but thank you kindly."

Davy pointed to the sack. "There's something else in there for you," he said.

Mike reached in again. This time he pulled out a big green felt hat with a bright red feather—exactly like the one he had eaten!

"Aw, you shouldn't have done it," he said.

"Georgie and me didn't want nobody thinking you wasn't still King of the River," Davy said.

Mike proudly put the hat on his head. "Never was no danger of that!" he said. "You bushwhackers ever get a hankering to be rivermen again, just look me up."

With that, he turned to his crew and bellowed, "All right, get back to work, you fork-tailed scorpions! Set poles!"

The men all scrambled around to grab their poles. They plunged them into the water and pushed off. In seconds, the *Gullywhumper* was moving away from the riverbank.

Mike's orders echoed across the river. "Put your backs into it! Shove on them poles. What do you think this is, a pleasure cruise? We got a cargo to move!"

Davy and Georgie grinned at each other. It felt good to hear Mike yelling at someone else for a change.

As the *Gullywhumper* floated upriver, Davy and Georgie made their way into the woods. The trees were thick, but Davy spotted a place where some bushes had been cut away. "Hey, there's a trail," he said. "It ought to lead us right to a Chickasaw camp."

They walked along, stepping on pine needles and branches. The soft crunching beneath their feet was the only sound they heard.

Suddenly Davy stopped short. "What's the matter?" Georgie asked. "Did you hear something?"

"No," said Davy. "And that's exactly what's wrong."

Georgie listened carefully and nodded. "Yeah, you're right. Not a sound! Not even a bird or a squir-rel. Something must have scared them."

"Must be a Chickasaw hunting party nearby."

Georgie shrugged. "Well, they ain't hunting us. Let's find them."

"Reckon they'll find us if we stay on this trail." Davy started walking again. Suddenly his foot caught on something.

Davy looked down. "Hey, what's this—"

He didn't have a chance to finish the sentence. A rope tightened around his ankle and pulled him straight up into the air!

CHAPTER 2

**D**avy thrashed his arms. He was swinging upside down, five feet above the ground. "Hey, get me down!"

Georgie ran toward him, laughing. "So, you stepped in an old deer snare, huh? What'd folks say if they could see the King of the Wild Frontier now, hey?"

"Just cut me down!" Davy shouted.

Georgie chuckled as he reached for his pocketknife. Then, *he* felt something pull at *his* leg.

"Yeeeeeaaaaagh!" he shouted, as he was yanked off his feet. Now, Georgie and Davy were both hanging upside down, helpless.

Slowly the bushes around them began to rustle and move. A feather popped out from behind one. Then a face. Then two more faces.

Soon Davy and Georgie were surrounded by Chickasaws. Angry-looking Chickasaws, wearing war paint on their faces.

The Chickasaws cut Davy and Georgie down. Then, moving quickly, they used the ropes to bind Davy's and Georgie's hands and feet.

"What's going on here?" Davy called out. "We're friends!"

"Yeah, you're making a terrible mistake!" Georgie added. "Can't you see that's Davy Crockett you're trying to hog-tie?"

Stone faced, the Indians spoke to each other in the Chickasaw language.

"Davy, they're not listening to us," Georgie said. There was panic in his voice.

"Just do whatever they want," Davy said.

Davy and Georgie were each shoved onto a horse. The Chickasaws led them, single file, down a path that wound its way through the forest for miles, along the bank of a narrow river.

After about an hour of traveling silently in this manner, one of the Chickasaws shouted what sounded like a command. The men stopped their horses and dismounted. Two Chickasaws helped Davy and Georgie off their horses and loosened the ropes around their legs just enough so they could walk.

"Mighty generous of you," Georgie said.

He and Davy walked slowly to the river. Their arms were still tied, so they had to lay on their stomachs to take a drink.

"I thought the Chickasaws was so all-fire friendly,"

Georgie grumbled. "Where in tarnation are they taking us?"

"Don't know," Davy replied. "Something mighty bad must have happened if the Chickasaw Indians have formed war parties."

Georgie looked over his shoulder. The Chickasaws were looking away, tending to the horses. "Let's make a break for it," he whispered. "We might never get another chance."

Suddenly a shadow loomed over them. They turned and looked up at a Chickasaw warrior, armed with a bow and arrow.

"What makes you think we got a chance *now*, Georgie?" Davy said.

The warrior waved toward the horses. Davy and Georgie both knew that was a signal for them to get moving.

Before long, they were all riding the trail again. The horses slowly worked their way through the woods.

After another hour, they arrived at a clearing, where a few small huts surrounded an open fire. Two Chickasaw men pulled Davy and Georgie down from their horses and pushed them into one of the huts.

They tumbled to the floor and looked around, but there was nothing to see. The hut was completely empty. Outside they could hear the steady beat of drums and some loud Chickasaw conversation.

"Well, now you know where they was taking us," Davy said.

"Yeah, but what are they going to do with us?" Georgie asked.

"I don't know," Davy said. "But something tells me whatever it is ain't too friendly."

Just then the hut's front flap flew open. Two Indian men entered the hut. One was young and strong looking, like the men who had brought Davy and Georgie to the camp. But the other man was different. His face was old and weathered, his walk slow. There were dozens of feathers adorning the headdress that streamed down his back.

"Mind your manners, Georgie," Davy said. "This is the chief."

The old man's voice was deep and rumbly. He gave the younger brave some instructions in the Chickasaw language. But when he addressed Davy and Georgie, he spoke in clear English. "Chief Black Eagle is my name," he said. "I am told you are the hunter Davy Crockett."

"He sure is, Chief," Georgie replied.

"You are known to us as a friend," Black Eagle continued.

Looking straight at Davy, he said, "You and your friend will not be harmed."

Georgie was relieved. "That's right nice of you,

Chief. Well, we'd like to stay and jawbone awhile, but Davy and me's got to get going. . . ."

"But you will remain with us," Black Eagle said.

Georgie slumped with disappointment.

"Why are your men in red and black war paint?" Davy asked.

Black Eagle glared at him. "We go to avenge the murder of our brothers." He turned toward the other Indian. "This man is a messenger from the chief of the Kaskaskia tribe. Settlers have been killing his people without reason, hunting them down like animals."

"Kaskaskias," Davy repeated. "They're up on the Ohio River, around Cave-in Rock."

Cave-in Rock. Georgie recognized that name right away. That was where he and Davy had saved Mike Fink's life from an Indian ambush.

"Well, it's no wonder folks have been shooting at them," Georgie said. "They've been attacking every boat that comes down the river!"

Black Eagle turned to the Kaskaskia messenger again. "Do you understand what they say?"

"I understand, but they lie. It is our people who are being attacked," the messenger said. "We lived in peace along the river until the settlers began to make war on *us*."

"Now listen here, you!" Georgie said hotly. "We're telling the truth. We seen it, didn't we Davy?"

"Sure did," Davy replied.

Black Eagle narrowed his eyes at Davy. "When was this?"

"No more than three months ago," Davy said.

Georgie nodded. "Yeah, we helped break up a raid on a boat just below the big cave."

"More lies!" the messenger shot back. "Three moons ago, my people were hiding far from the river, driven deep into the woods by settlers."

"Hiding?" asked Davy.

"That means it must have been some other tribe," George said.

The messenger shook his head. "There are no other tribes in that land. And we have kept the peace."

"I believe you," Davy said. "Georgie, do you know what this means?"

Georgie was deep in thought. "Well, it could mean some skunks are dressing up like Indians, so the Kaskaskias get the blame, while the real pirates go free!"

That was exactly what Davy was thinking, too. He hadn't saved Mike from an Indian attack after all. He had saved him from a band of river pirates in costume!

Davy was angry. "Chief," he said. "We're going to find out who they are and put a stop to this!"

"How can we trust you?" the messenger replied.

Davy and Georgie looked to Black Eagle for a decision. Black Eagle's face was hard as stone. He spoke only four words and turned away.

"You will remain here."

**Y**ou say you know me!" Davy cried to Black Eagle. "Then you know my word is good. Give us a chance."

"We'll chase those varmints out into the open, guaranteed!" Georgie added.

"And if they ain't Indians, we'll see that everybody finds out," Davy said.

Black Eagle stopped at the entrance to the hut. Slowly he turned around. He fixed his eyes on Davy, then on Georgie. It was as if he were looking right through them, reading their minds.

"It is too late," he finally said. "Already war messengers have gone to the Shawnees, the Miamis, the Kickapoos, and the Chippewas."

"Then call them back," Davy said. "Send out runners of your own. Tell the chiefs to keep the peace, at least until we can investigate."

"Know this, Davy Crockett," Black Eagle replied sharply. "We have always wanted peace. But the settlers do not want peace with us. They make treaties and break them whenever they please. They call us brother but believe any evil they hear of us."

"That may be true in some cases, Chief," said Davy. "But it works two ways. To strike back at a few no-good, murdering river pirates, you're willing to turn the whole frontier into a needless battleground. Think of how many innocent people will die—your people included."

Black Eagle fell silent again, letting Davy's words sink in. Then he nodded his head and said, "I will send runners to call off the war."

Davy and Georgie started to thank him, but he held up his hand to silence them. "But not for long. I will instruct my warriors to wait only until the next full moon. If you do not succeed by then, we will go to war."

He turned and shouted orders. Two tribesmen came in and untied Davy and Georgie.

"Thank you, fellas," Davy said. "Now come on, Georgie. We got some work to do."

As they ran out of the hut, Georgie said, "Where in tarnation are we going?"

"To head off the *Gullywhumper!*" Davy replied.

Outside, two Chickasaw men were sitting on horses,

listening to commands from Black Eagle. The old chief turned to Davy and Georgie and said, "Red River and Setting Sun will take you wherever you need to go."

"Thanks, Chief," Davy said. He and Georgie hopped up behind their guides. "Ask him if he knows a shortcut to the Ohio River."

Black Eagle addressed his men again. They nodded, then kicked their horses into motion.

It took them two hours to reach a steep hill in the midst of the forest. The Chickasaws pointed up the hill, let Davy and Georgie dismount, and then took off.

It was almost nighttime. Davy knew they had to move fast before it was too dark to see.

They scrambled up the hill. There, stretched out below them, was the Ohio River.

"Sure hope that old *Gullywhumper* didn't pass this way before we got here," Georgie said.

"They ain't had time, poling upriver against the current," Davy replied. "We got a long way ahead of them, thanks to the Chickasaws."

"Davy, you sure old Mike's going to want to help us out?" Georgie asked.

"I know he will," Davy said. "I think he's proved he's a friend we can count on."

Georgie nodded. "Yeah, but the chief didn't give us much time. It won't take long for that moon to fatten up."

Davy looked up. The moon was just over the horizon, plump but not quite full. It shone down on a familiar outline making its way up the river.

The *Gullywhumper*.

"Well," Davy said with a smile, "leastways we ain't going to waste no more time here."

They began to wave at Mike's boat, but then Davy spotted a canoe, near the opposite riverbank, silently making its way toward the *Gullywhumper*. On it were three Chickasaw men, their faces painted for war!

# CHAPTER 4

**D**avy ducked. "Get down!" He grabbed Georgie's arm and pulled him to the ground.

"What's the matter with you?" Georgie asked.

Davy pointed to the Chickasaw canoe. "That's what's the matter, Georgie."

Georgie's eyes widened. "It's a group of warriors. I thought the chief had called them all off."

"I guess Black Eagle's runners didn't warn this bunch," Davy said.

"Now what?" Georgie asked.

Davy looked around. In the dim moonlight, he could make out the shape of another canoe. It was almost hidden behind some trees at the edge of the river. Davy could see two Chickasaws, deeper in the woods, heading toward the canoe.

"We're going to get a boat and warn Mike," Davy said simply.

He quickly raced down the hill, with Georgie right behind. They snuck up to the canoe and waited.

The woods rustled to their left. The Chickasaws were getting closer and closer. . . .

Suddenly Davy and Georgie sprang into action. They grabbed the two men and wrestled them to the ground.

Moments later, Davy and Georgie were rowing down the Ohio, dressed in full Chickasaw costume, in case they encountered any more Indians. They plunged their oars in and sped toward the *Gullywhumper* while the canoe with the real Chickasaws rowed closer and closer to Mike's boat from the other side.

"Hey, Mike!" Georgie called out.

Because Georgie was shouting into the wind, Mike couldn't hear him. Davy and Georgie could hear Mike though. "It's an Indian attack, boys!" he cried. "They're all around us. Jocko, get below and get the new cannon!"

Davy and Georgie rowed harder. They could see Mike and Jocko rolling the cannon over to the side of the boat they were rowing toward.

"Hey, Mike!" Georgie tried again.

But they were still too far away for Mike to hear them. He struck a match and lit the cannon's fuse. It began to spit sparks.

"Hey, Mike, wait! *Wait!*"

*Kabooooooom!*

A cannonball shot through the night air. With a

loud splash, it landed in the water, a few feet from Davy and Georgie's canoe.

Davy and Georgie hung on as the small boat rocked. They heard Mike shouting, "Come on. Load up!"

"*Mike!*" Georgie tried again, at the top of his lungs. "It's me and Davy!"

They heard the loud cracks of gunshot aimed at the other canoe. Swiftly the Chickasaws retreated toward the shore.

Mike roared with laughter. "Look, boys! They're on the run!" He grabbed the cannon himself and pointed it at Davy and Georgie. "Haw! Haw! Haw! This is more fun than shooting catfish!"

Georgie waved his arms wildly. "Hey, we're not Chickasaws!"

Suddenly, Jocko grabbed Mike's arm. He was staring at Davy and Georgie. "Hey, hey, Mike, ain't that—"

Mike pushed him aside. "Stop it! You're ruining my aim!"

Now Davy and Georgie were both standing and waving their arms. "Stop shooting, Mike!" Georgie yelled.

"But, Mike," Jocko insisted, "it looks like—"

"Quit shoving, will you?" Mike shouted.

*Kabooooooom!* The cannon went off again.

Davy and Georgie jumped out of the canoe as the cannonball barreled right into it. With an ear-splitting sound, the canoe exploded into bits!

CHAPTER 5

**D**avy and Georgie floated in the water, their heads bobbing on the surface. Jagged pieces of wood were scattered all around them. They had jumped ship just in time.

On the *Gullywhumper,* Mike squinted at them. Hunkered down by the cannon, he slowly rose to his full height. "Well, what do you know? It's them two varmints, Crockett and Russel!"

"Mike, you bullheaded, trigger-happy baboon!" Georgie cried.

Mike turned around to his crew. "Pole, you fools! Can't you see we got men overboard?"

The *Gullywhumper* crew poled the boat closer to Davy and Georgie. Jocko and Mike reached down and hoisted Davy aboard.

But Georgie turned and swam away.

"Hey, where are you going?" Jocko called. He looked at Davy, baffled. "Something wrong with him?"

"He's a little angry, Jocko," Davy said. "I'll go handle it."

"I'll meet you down in the cabin," Mike said.

Davy ran around to the back of the boat. Looking down, he saw Georgie treading water, a scowl on his face.

"Come back and make up with Mike," Davy coaxed. "He didn't mean it, and you know it."

"No sir, I ain't going to do it!" Georgie retorted.

"Oh, quit your fussing, Georgie. How'd he know we wasn't Chickasaw warriors?"

"That ain't no excuse  Why he shot at us with our own present! He might have got us killed!"

"You sure are stoved up, ain't you?" Davy let out a sigh. "Well, I guess we'll have to make plans all by ourselves."

He walked back along the deck and climbed down the stairs to the main cabin. When Mike saw him, he said with a laugh, "So, old Georgie forgive me yet?"

Davy shook his head. "No, but he'll get over it."

"Well, long as it was just his feelings got hurt," Mike said. "Now, tell me why did you fellas come out here anyways? You miss us or something?"

Davy told him what had happened at the Chickasaw camp. He explained his suspicions about the pirates near Shawneetown.

Mike listened carefully. "You know, Davy," he

said, "you showed rare good sense in getting old Mike Fink to help you. Me and my skull busters will make mincemeat out of them!"

"Yeah, but we have to find them first," Davy reminded him.

"Well, I ain't certain they'll show themselves after that beating I gave them coming downriver," Mike said proudly. "They're sure to recognize the old *Gullywhumper*!"

Jocko interrupted the conversation. "Hey, Mike! Look what's coming!"

Davy and Mike ran up the stairs. Jocko was pointing to a dark, motionless keelboat in the middle of the river.

"Why, that's the *Monongahela Belle*," Mike said.

"Where's her crew?" Davy asked.

"That's what I aim to find out," Mike told him grimly. Then he called over his shoulder, "Prepare to grab her as she comes alongside, boys!"

The *Gullywhumper* floated smoothly up to the other boat. Jocko and several other crewmen grabbed onto its railing. They brought the boats together so their sides were just touching.

"All right, hold her tight, you scummy river rats!" Mike commanded.

He and Davy climbed over the two boats' railings and boarded the *Monongahela Belle*.

"If anybody's here, they're in the cabin," Mike said.

The cabin door was open, and Mike bounded loudly down the stairs.

But Davy stayed on deck. He had noticed something sticking in the door.

A tomahawk.

CHAPTER 6

**M**ike came slowly back up the stairs. He had re- moved his hat and was holding it in his hands. "I knowed old Cap Donovan," he said, softly. "Looks like he put up a real good fight before they wiped him out."

Davy was examining the tomahawk. "No Indian ever made this," he said.

Suddenly an arm reached around Davy and grabbed the tomahawk!

Davy spun around. There was Georgie, sopping wet, holding the tomahawk up so that the moonlight re- flected on the blade. "Yeah, you're right. Ain't no tribal markings, and it ain't feathered right. I wonder how far downstream she drifted since the massacre?"

"There ain't no way of telling," Mike answered.

"There might be some clues downstairs," Davy sug- gested.

They went back down to the cabin. Their footsteps

echoed in the quiet main room. It was almost completely empty. There was a spilled cup of coffee on the floor, a pair of broken eyeglasses, and a half-eaten plate of beef stew on a countertop. Davy felt a shiver go up his spine.

"They didn't hardly leave nothing," said Mike.

"Well, they left these," Davy said, pointing to a jumble of clothes, heaped in a corner. He rummaged through them, thinking. Then he picked up a dark business suit and held it out to Mike. "Try this on for size," he said.

"What!" Mike sneered. "I wouldn't be caught dead in a monkey suit like that. What's it even doing here?"

"I don't know," said Davy, "but I have a plan. We're going to set a trap for these no-good river pirates and that means we have to disguise you and the *Gullywhumper*. If they recognize you, they'll remember the whuppin' they got last time, and they'll stay away. Now put it on, Mike! If you want to be a hero, sometimes you got to do things you don't want to do."

Grumbling, Mike put on the suit. He stood up tall and said, "Goldarnit, I look like a dadblamed banker!"

Georgie doubled over with laughter. "I tell you one thing. I'd think twice about giving you any of my money."

Mike clenched his fists and glared at Georgie. "Remember, Mike," Davy said, "you're a banker. Act like a banker. Control yourself. Act dignified."

Mike unclenched his fists, adjusted his jacket, and walked stiffly up the stairs.

The sight of Mike in a suit was enough to crack up Davy, too. But Davy held it in. Too bad the rest of the *Gullywhumper* crew couldn't do the same. "Hoooo-ha-ha-ha-ha-ha!" Jocko blurted as Mike stepped on deck.

Jocko's partner, Moose, joined in. Soon the whole river was echoing with laughter.

"If you pea-brained hyenas don't get this boat to shore in five minutes, I'll personally tan each and every one of your hides!" Mike bellowed. "I want this old tank disguised in half an hour!"

The crew poled the boat to the riverbank. They set up a plank from the deck to the shore, then teetered down it. While a team of men gave the *Gullywhumper* a new coat of paint, Georgie carefully painted the name *Bonanza* on the side.

On deck, Mike rolled the cannon toward Moose. "Hide this below, where we can get to it in a hurry," he ordered.

As Moose disappeared into the cabin with the cannon, Mike spotted Jocko walking up the plank. Jocko was carrying a heavy, lumpy sack. Mike lay down on his stomach and reached down to help him up. "What's so heavy in that sack?" he asked.

"Rocks," Jocko answered.

"*Rocks?*" Mike let go, and Jocko tumbled backward into the water with a big splash. "You feather-headed idiot! I never heard anything so dumb as lugging bags of rocks aboard a keelboat!"

Out of the corner of his eye, Mike could see Davy and Georgie filling more sacks with rocks. "What's going on here?" Mike questioned angrily. He leapt to the shore, shouting, "What in thunderation are you up to?"

Davy turned to him. "Well, you're a banker, ain't you?" he asked calmly.

"Yes, sir," Mike said. "King of the Bankers, that's me. On my way up to Shawneetown to open up a new establishment. But what's these here rocks got to do with that?"

"You can't run a bank without money, can you?" asked Davy.

"No, I don't reckon," Mike said. "But—"

Georgie held up his sack of rocks. "It's your capital, genuine Spanish gold."

Mike caught on. The sacks were going to be part of the plan to trick the pirates. "Say. . . ." he said with a smile, picking up a rock. "We're rich, ain't we?"

"Well, that's what we're hoping them pirates will think," Davy said. "I figure we can stop in a couple of towns to spread rumors about our rich cargo. Then word ought to get upriver faster than we can."

"Good thinking," Mike said. "That ought to flush out them pirates."

It seemed like a perfect plan.

**CHAPTER**

For more than an hour the crew poled while Mike stood at the tiller and steered. Finally the lights of a river town shone in the distance.

"Say, Davy, take over," Mike called out. " 'Tain't fitting for a banker to be seen steering his own boat."

"You bet," Davy said. He grabbed the tiller and steered the *Gullywhumper* into a cove. After they docked, the whole *Gullywhumper* crew walked into town.

At the foot of the main street, there was a party being held under a large striped tent. Dozens of townspeople laughed and ate and danced to fiddle music.

A well-dressed man was clapping to the music by the front of the tent. When he saw Mike approach, he said, "Welcome, fellas!"

"Fiddle player's got real talent," Mike remarked.

The fiddle player heard him and smiled.

"Oh yes," the well-dressed man replied. "He hits

this town every once in a while. Plays to drum up business for himself."

"Who is he?" Davy asked.

"A peddler from back East," the man said. "Calls himself Colonel Plug."

"Yes, indeed, that's some mighty admiral . . . admirab . . . admire . . . er, fancy playing," Mike said, trying hard to sound intelligent.

Georgie poked Mike in the ribs. *"Admirable,"* he murmured.

"Allow me to introduce myself," the man said. He held out his hand to Mike. "I'm the magistrate here in Freeport. I don't believe I got your name, stranger."

"Uh, Magillicuddy," Mike said, shaking the magistrate's hand. "J. J. Magillicuddy, on my way to Shawneetown to open up a new bank."

Davy and Georgie kept their lips tight, to keep from laughing.

The magistrate was still looking at Mike, though. He looked worried. "Mister Magillicuddy, I feel it my duty to inform you that river travel is not safe up here on the Ohio anymore."

Mike smiled confidently and said, "Well, if you're referring to them Indian pirates, we ain't carrying nothing they'd want. No guns, no gunpowder, not even any whiskey." Then he cleared his throat and announced in a loud voice, "Yep. All's we got is a cargo of old Spanish gold."

*Sproingggg!* Suddenly a string broke on the fiddle, and the music stopped. The fiddle player, along with everyone else within earshot, stared at Mike.

"A cargo of gold!" the magistrate exclaimed. "Why, I'm surprised that your captain would risk that."

"Well, uh, um . . ." Mike struggled for a second before turning to Davy. "You ain't scared any, are you, Cap?"

"Not about the gold," Davy said.

"We'll believe them Indians when we see them," Georgie chimed in.

"They're real, all right," the magistrate said. "Wrecks of boats drift by all the time. Plenty of bodies are fished out of the water."

"No use to try and scare us off, Mister," Davy said.

"We've been hearing them Indian stories all the way up from New Orleans," Georgie added. "Buncha tall tales if you ask me."

"Listen, you know who Mike Fink is, don't you?" the magistrate asked.

Davy shrugged. "Never heard of him. Who's he?"

"Mike Fink," the magistrate said. "Calls himself King of the River."

"Oh, that big blowhard," Georgie replied. "What about him?"

Mike glared at Georgie. "Yeah, what about him?"

"Why, I've heard that even he's going to quit the river," the magistrate said.

"You heard *what?*" Mike retorted.

The magistrate nodded. "Yes sir, even that braying jackass is too scared to risk it."

"*Jackass?*" Mike roared.

"Now, Mr. Magillicuddy," Davy warned, "don't go getting yourself in a lather."

Mike's face was red. His eyes were practically popping out of his head. "You . . . why . . . I . . . I'll . . ." he sputtered. Then, catching Davy's glance, he swallowed hard. He straightened out his jacket and shut his mouth.

"It's okay," Georgie explained to the magistrate. "It's only one of his nervous fits."

Just then the fiddle player, Colonel Plug, stepped down off his platform. "Excuse me, Mr. Magillicuddy," he said, "I couldn't help overhearing, but do you really intend on going farther upriver?"

Mike exhaled hard, pulling himself together. Georgie's last remark had nearly set him off again. "You don't think I'd go this far otherwise, now do you?" he replied soberly, watching Plug's face.

Plug smiled. "Well now, I admire a man of courage. Just so happens I'm mighty anxious to get on up to Shawneetown myself."

"We're pretty crowded already," Davy said.

"Aw, shucks, I don't take up much room," Plug answered. "All I got is my case and my fiddle."

Mike looked at Davy. "A little music wouldn't hurt none, would it?"

"This ain't no pleasure cruise," Davy said. "I'm afraid Mr. Plug'll have to wait here for another riverboat."

"Listen," Mike retorted, "you may be the captain, but I'm the boss banker of this outfit, ain't I? Well, I say he goes with us!"

And that was that.

A few minutes later, as Plug boarded the *Gully-whumper* with the rest of the crew, two men watched from behind a large rock.

"Did Plug get aboard this one?" the bigger man asked.

"Yeah, just went into the cabin," said the other. He spelled out the letters on the side of the boat: "B-O-N-A-N-Z-A. Ever hear of her?"

"You know I can't spell," the first man snarled.

Back on the *Gullywhumper*, Plug pulled his fiddle out of its case. "Say, fellas," he said, "I got a new verse I want to try out on Mister Magillicuddy."

As Plug tuned up, Georgie whispered to Davy, "Something mighty fishy about that peddler. Why'd you let Mike bring him aboard?"

" 'Cause he's the first sucker that nibbled at our bait," Davy told him.

Then Plug began to sing very loudly. It was a tune familiar to the two men on shore. It meant there was gold on board.

"Come on," said the bigger man, "we got work to do."

Their horses were hidden behind a grove of trees. The two men mounted quickly and disappeared into the woods.

CHAPTER 8

**B**uried in the woods, a stone's throw from Freeport, was the Cave-in Club. It had a great view of the Ohio and a roaring fire inside. You might say it was the most exclusive club in town. Most people didn't even know about it.

If the Cave-in Club had a motto, it would be Only the Worst. The local cutthroats, purse snatchers, horse thieves, train robbers, river pirates—all of them showed up there, night after night.

Bloody Sam Mason, the owner of the place, was the worst of them all. Most nights he stayed in a back room of the club, concocting nasty plans with his henchmen—a man named Fiddler and two brothers named Harpe.

Piracy was what they did best. And they were experts at pinning the blame on others.

Like the Kaskaskia Indians.

In the back room of the club, there were chests full of Indian clothing, weapons, wigs, and jars of war paint.

Some of the stuff had been stolen from the Kaskaskias. The rest were fakes. Mason's men would disguise themselves as Kaskaskias before attacking boats along the Ohio.

The night of the Freeport tent fair, the Cave-in Club was jammed full. Men laughed, fought, broke glasses, and sang. Mason wandered through the room, keeping an eye out for the Harpe brothers.

When they came into the club, Mason could tell something was up. "More business for us?" he asked.

The Harpes both grinned. They were good spies, but they weren't very smart. In fact, they were so dumb they couldn't even remember their own first names! People called them Little Harpe and Big Harpe.

"Yeah," Little Harpe answered Mason. "It's a real rich one this time. And Plug's already aboard!"

"Good," Mason said. "What's her cargo?"

"Gold," Little Harpe replied, his eyes wide.

" 'Yeller, yeller gold!' " Big Harpe said. "That's what Plug was singing."

Mason's face twisted into a gap-toothed smile. "Mighty obliging of them to ship it our way," he said. "What's the name of this boat?"

"It ain't the *Gullywhumper*, if that's what's bothering you," Little Harpe said, remembering the strange name painted on the side.

Mason flinched at the mention of the *Gullywhumper*. It was only about three months ago that his men had attacked her. And it was the only time they had ever been defeated. "Quit rubbing that in!" Mason snapped. "Mike Fink wouldn't have got away if I'd been with you. We ain't had no trouble since, have we?"

"Naw," Big Harpe said, "just a lot of fun!"

The three of them burst into laughter. They always felt best before a big ambush.

"T his waiting for something to happen is making me nervous," Georgie said, pacing the deck. "Time is getting short. That moon is filling out real fast."

Davy scanned the tree-lined banks of the river. His right hand gripped the tiller. He turned it ever so slightly, making sure the boat wasn't too close to the land. In the darkness, he had to be extra careful. "Well, we still got a few days," he said softly.

"Yeah, but it's going to take a few days just to get word back to the Chickasaws," Georgie reminded him.

"I don't reckon we've got long to wait now," Davy answered.

They heard Mike's heavy footsteps. "My boys is all ready," he said. "Chock-full of fight and itching to get at 'em."

"Not so loud," Georgie whispered. "We don't want Colonel Plug to hear."

"Aw, he's still sleeping," Mike said.

"Better make sure." Davy got up from the tiller. "Take over, Mr. Magillicuddy. This here is called a tiller."

Mike sat down and took his place. Davy quietly opened the cabin door and made his way downstairs. He walked along the narrow hallway toward the sleeping quarters. When he found Plug's room, he slowly opened the door and peeked in. Plug was fast asleep.

Or so Davy thought.

The minute he closed the door, Plug's eyes sprang open. Plug listened carefully as Davy walked back up the stairs. When he heard the cabin door shut, he leapt out of bed.

From under his bed, he pulled out a hand drill, two small hooks, a string, and a cork. Quietly he lifted the drill, stuck it into his wall, and began to turn it.

After a dozen turns—*chhsssss!* Water started to spray into the room. Plug yanked the drill out, then plugged the cork into the hole.

The water stopped spurting. Plug smiled. His plan was beginning to take shape.

He looked up at a window in the opposite wall. On the other side of that wall was Moose's room. Plug could hear him snoring peacefully.

Working fast, Plug tied a hook onto either end of the string. He screwed one of the hooks into the cork. Then he pulled the other hooked end of the string all the way to the window.

He threaded that end through a crack in the window. Ever so slowly, he lowered the hook down toward Moose. It caught on the back of Moose's shirt. Plug gave a quick pull to make sure it was stuck.

Moose was so fast asleep, he never even felt it.

Step one of Plug's plan was finished. The minute Moose awoke and got out of bed, he'd pull out the cork and the boat would start to flood. That still left Plug enough time for step two—finding the gold. When Mason's men attacked, he'd toss it to them and jump overboard. That would be the third and final step.

He snuck into the hallway, looking left and right. At the end of it was a closed door that was marked Storage Hold. That had to be the place.

Tiptoeing, he went to the door and pushed it open. He reached into his pocket, took out a match, and struck it.

As the room lit up, so did Plug's eyes. There were bags and bags, all of them bulging. He'd never seen so much money. He wondered how much he could pocket without telling Mason.

He pulled open one of the bags and dug his hand inside.

His face froze. Then his smile turned into an angry scowl. "Rocks," he said under his breath. "Just plain rocks!"

He opened another bag, then another. Then his eyes lit on something else—a cannon. He held a match close to it and read the inscription. "Mike Fink!" he said in a shocked whisper. "Davy Crockett!"

He had been tricked. Mason and the gang were walking into a trap. Furious, Plug ran back into the hallway. Stopping in his room to pick up his fiddle, he bolted upstairs.

Up on the deck, Mike took off his suit jacket. "This is about the place they jumped us before," he said. "And I've worn this monkey suit long enough!"

As Mike tossed his jacket overboard, Plug came bounding onto the deck. "Uh, excuse me, boys," he said. "I . . . I was having a little trouble getting to sleep. I thought maybe you fellas might like to hear some music."

Without waiting for an answer, he started strumming his fiddle. Then he turned to the riverbank and sang away at the top of his lungs to warn Mason's gang that instead of "yeller gold" there was a cannon waiting for them!

CHAPTER
10

The Harpe brothers were hidden in a small clearing in the woods, just a few feet from the shore, waiting for a sight of the disguised *Gullywhumper*.

"That sounded like Plug," Big Harpe said, when the song reached their ears. "Why's he still singing?"

"What difference does it make now?" Little Harpe answered.

Big Harpe nodded. "You're right," he said. The brothers were too foolish to even listen to Plug's warning!

But back on the *Gullywhumper*, the entire crew heard Plug's words and knew right away what he was up to. Jocko slapped his hand over Plug's mouth. Davy grabbed the fiddle and threw it overboard. The two of them pulled Plug down into the cabin while Georgie followed with a strong rope.

Plug kicked and twisted, but Davy and Jocko held tight. Georgie threw the rope around Plug and began to tie him up.

At the top of the stairs, Mike called down, "Hey, Davy, I see we're about to get visitors! Bring a *present* for them when you come up!"

Davy knew what that meant. Mike had spotted some attackers and wanted Davy to bring the cannon up on deck.

"Let's move!" Davy shouted. He and Georgie threw Plug into his room, bound and gagged. In their haste they left the door open.

As they ran to the storage room, they could hear Mike again. "Hey, Moose!" he shouted. "Come aft and be gunner!"

"Hrrrargghh!" Moose mumbled. He rolled slowly out of bed and stood up. As he walked out of the room, he didn't even notice that his shirt was pulling Plug's string.

In the next room, Plug noticed. His eyes were wide with fear, staring at the cork inching its way out of his wall. He tried to shout, but the rag in his mouth muffled the sound.

*Spurk!*

The cork popped. Water gushed into Plug's room, splashing against his face.

His plan had worked—but not in the way he had wanted it to!

On deck, Mike was getting ready to fight. He threw his starched collar down on the deck. "Pole that way, boys!" he shouted to his crew. "I see 'em in the bushes!"

Jocko and the rest of the crew poled as hard as they could. At the riverbank, Mason's men were pulling off the tree branches that hid their canoes. Behind them, Mason had joined the Harpe brothers. They sat on their horses, watching.

Davy and Georgie pulled the cannon up the stairs and rolled it to the railing. Davy pointed it at Mason's men. "They're too far away," he told Mike. "If we want a good shot, we've got to get closer."

But the *Gullywhumper* seemed to be slowing down. "You clodhoppers taking a break or something?" Mike ranted. "Close in on them!"

"What do you think we're trying to do?" Jocko yelled back.

Davy turned and looked. Jocko was right. The men were poling harder than ever, but the boat hardly seemed to be moving.

"Mike!" Jocko suddenly shouted. "We're dragging bottom!"

"Well, it's them confounded rocks you brought aboard!" Mike said. "Get them out of here!"

"I'll go," Moose volunteered, and he opened the cabin door.

But he took only a few steps before he slipped. With a loud splash, he plunged into water nearly up to his chest.

"What the—?" Moose looked around in shock. Through the open door to Plug's room, he could see water streaming in from the hole in the wall. He saw the cork, attached to the string, floating on the water, and with his eyes he followed the string through the window to his room and saw the other end of the string—hooked to a ripped piece of his own shirt.

Moose could not believe his eyes. He swam quickly back to the stairs, ignoring Plug. "We're sinking, Mike!" he bellowed.

From the deck, Mike stared in horror at the scene below, then at the approaching canoes. "Sinking?" he cried out. "We're sunk!"

# CHAPTER 11

**M**oose was purple with anger. Clenching his fists, he sloshed through the water back to Plug.

"You did this, didn't you?" he growled, picking up Plug by the front of his shirt. "You put that hook in my shirt!"

Plug jerked his body left and right, trying to loosen his ropes. He was afraid that Moose was going to hurt him. "Mmmmrrrffff!" he mumbled.

Moose yanked the gag out of Plug's mouth.

"What're you tryin' to say, you no-good thieving pirate?" he demanded.

"Let me go! Let me go!" Plug shouted. "I'll have the law on you!"

Moose laughed. "You'll have the law on *me?*" he said. He lifted Plug higher, right up to a big metal hook on the wall. He hooked the back of Plug's pants on it, so that now at least Plug would not drown.

"I'll have the law on you!" Plug kept yelling as he

dangled helplessly. But Moose just ran back upstairs. He knew he'd be needed there.

He was right. Mike was pushing the cannon into place and shouting, "Grab your weapons, boys, and let 'em have it!"

Mason's men were closing in. There were at least six canoes, filled with river pirates disguised as Indians, racing toward the *Gullywhumper*.

The entire crew sprang into action. Moose rushed over to help Mike. Davy and Georgie aimed their rifles. The polers lifted their poles, ready to strike.

*Crrraack! Crrraack!*

Davy and Georgie fired. The bullets hit one of the canoes. With yelps of surprise, three men fell overboard.

*Kabooooooom!* went Mike's cannon. The cannonball hurtled through the air and landed with a huge splash in front of the advancing canoes.

The canoes bounced wildly in the wake of the splash. Many men went flying into the water.

"Yeee-*haaahhh!*" Georgie shouted.

"Get the powder!" Mike yelled to Moose. "Come on, fill 'er up!"

Some of Mason's men were now heading toward them, fighting against the river's current. "Come on, guys, let's get 'em!" shouted one of the *Gullywhumper* crewmen.

Three of the crew dived into the water. Fists began to fly, and water splashed everywhere. More and more men jumped into the fray.

Jocko stood on the deck, holding his pole. He wanted to swing, but it was hard to tell who was who in the darkness.

Finally one of the "Kaskaskias" emerged right underneath him. Jocko swung as hard as he could.

The man ducked and the pole whooshed through the air.

"Whoooooa!" The weight of the pole as it swung around pulled Jocko over the railing. He plunged into the water.

*Kaboooooooooom!* The cannon went off again. Two more canoes upended, toppling more men into the water.

"Haw! Haw! Haw! Haw!" Mike laughed, clutching his belly with one hand and leaning on the cannon with the other.

Behind him, water was slowly seeping up from the cabin. Soon it began pooling around Mike's feet. The cannon's wheels began to slip—and so did Mike. "Goldang it!" Mike cried, as he and the cannon crashed through the railing and tumbled into the river.

Mike came to the surface with his fists flying. Around him, the water was swarming with battling men. Shouts and grunts mixed with the sound of splashing water. Men fought in the water, and they fought from the canoes. They climbed onto the *Gullywhumper* and fought some more.

And the whole time, they were all being watched from a distance. Sitting safely on their horses, up on a

cliff, Mason and the Harpe brothers were getting rest-
less.

Big Harpe shook his head with frustration. "Them
boatmen's putting up an awful good fight."

"We'll fix that," Mason said. "Get the powder keg
in the canoe."

"You can't use that now!" Little Harpe said. "You'd
blow up our own men!"

Mason's lips curled into a sneer. He let out a sinis-
ter laugh. "So what? It won't hurt *us* none!"

The three of them ran down the cliff and into a
small cove. In a canoe, hidden there by the trees, was a
gunpowder keg with a long fuse.

Mason stole a glance at the *Gullywhumper*. Mike's
crew was throwing molasses barrels off the side now,
hurling them at the attackers. Some of the barrels spilled
on deck, and people were slipping left and right.

"Perfect timing," Mason said gleefully. "Nobody
will even see it."

The three of them waded into the water. They
pushed the canoe into the open, then pointed it at the
*Gullywhumper*.

Mason pulled a match out of his pocket. "Ready?"
he asked.

"Ready," the Harpe brothers echoed.

Mason struck the match and held it to the fuse. It
burst into flame, and the three of them gave the canoe
one final push.

# CHAPTER 12

**G**eorgie could hardly stand. After all the punching and falling and throwing and ducking and swallowing water, he was worn out. Still, he knew he had enough fight left for any attacker who came his way.

But none of them were. They were all running away.

He watched them splashing toward the riverbank, practically falling over each other in their rush. "Yahoo!" he crowed. "We got them on the run!"

"No wonder," said Davy, beside him. "Look what's coming."

Davy pointed toward the shore. The powder keg was floating slowly toward them, its fuse spitting bright sparks into the air.

Georgie's jaw dropped. "Uh-oh. . . ."

"Come on, Georgie, grab a pole!" Davy cried.

They both picked up poles that were lying nearby and gently poked the powder keg canoe. Slowly they nudged it until it changed direction. With a final push, they sent it back toward the shore.

By that time, Mason and the Harpes had started swimming toward the *Gullywhumper*. They wanted to be able to grab the gold in a hurry when the boat began to sink.

But now the booby-trapped canoe was heading right for them and they knew it. Their arms flailed. Trying to turn around, they kicked and dunked each other under the water.

"They ain't going to make it," Georgie remarked.

He was right. The canoe was moving too fast. "Duck!" Mason screamed.

Three heads disappeared under the water as the powder keg exploded in a volcano of sparks and splinters.

"Somebody's been playing awful rough," Mike said, climbing over the railing.

Mike, Davy, and Georgie searched the water as the wreckage fell around them. Their brows were creased with concern. "Did they—?" Georgie began.

He didn't need to finish the sentence. The three men poked their heads above the surface, swam furiously to shore, and scrambled into the bushes.

But they didn't disappear before Mike recognized them. "Why, that's Sam Mason and the Harpe brothers," Mike said. "They're the orneriest skunks on the river!"

"And they're getting away!" Georgie said angrily.

"Oh no they ain't," Davy said. "You and me'll run them varmints down. Come on."

Davy and Georgie dived overboard. With powerful strokes, they reached the shore in seconds.

But the men were gone.

"What do we do now?" Georgie said. "It's too dark to see tracks. For all's we know, they could be waiting to ambush us in the woods."

"Well, if we wait till tomorrow's daylight, we may never find them," Davy said. Georgie was right though. It was impossible even to see a path into the deep woods.

Still, there was no other choice. With a deep sigh, Davy led the way in through the tree branches.

# CHAPTER 13

**P**anting heavily, Mason finally stopped running when he reached the entrance to the Cave-in Club. The Harpe brothers almost plowed into him from behind.

Mason knew the boatmen would try to find him. He had to gather up whatever loot he could carry easily and get lost until the coast was clear again.

"Big Harpe, you stay here and keep watch," Mason ordered.

"Wait a minute," Big Harpe protested, "what about my share?"

"Shut up and do like I told you. You'll get what's coming to you," said Mason roughly.

Big Harpe stayed put. Mason and Little Harpe ran through the cave and into the big main room. It was deserted, the night's party being over, and tables and chairs were scattered all over the place. The only light came from the lit fireplace and some wall torches.

They ran through the main room and into the back

room. This was a small room, crammed with bags, chests, and barrels full of loot from years and years of stealing.

Little Harpe began scooping up bags of money. Holding them in one hand, he reached for a wooden treasure chest.

"Leave the big stuff," Mason said. "We can't carry that on horseback."

Mason held out a huge sack, and Little Harpe stuffed it with loot. "Okay, that's enough for now," Mason said.

"We can't leave the rest of this for somebody else!" Little Harpe complained.

"Nobody's going to find it before we get back," Mason said.

Mason pointed to several large barrels to his right. "See those powder kegs? We'll set them up in the main room and run a trail of powder outside. Then we'll hide in the woods and wait for those water rats to find the place. When they get inside, we'll cave the place in. They'll be trapped, and our gold will be safe."

"Yeah, but then how will we get to it?" Little Harpe wanted to know.

"Use your head, you nitwit," Mason snapped. "We'll pay off a few of our fellas to help us dig through. Now come on, let's set it up."

They rolled the kegs into the main room. Mason

gathered loose rocks, crates, and small barrels. He piled them in front of the powder kegs to hide them. Little Harpe found a small shovel and dug some powder out of one of the kegs. He dribbled a trail from each keg out into the passageway.

Suddenly there were footsteps behind him. He whirled around to see Big Harpe. He looked panicked. "Somebody's coming up the trail!" he gasped.

"Grab one of these tools and get out of sight!" Mason ordered. Mason grabbed an ax, Little Harpe picked up a shovel, and Big Harpe took a hammer and a curved, wooden-handled blade. They quickly hid behind the powder kegs.


A few yards from the cave, Davy and Georgie paused. Using the dim moonlight, they had managed to find tracks. Now they were deep in the woods, and things were getting confusing.

"Too many tracks to tell which way they've gone," Davy said.

Georgie looked around. It looked like there were a half-dozen or so small caves tucked into the rocks. "They could be hiding in any one of these rat holes," he said.

"Say, Georgie, look!" Davy pointed to the sign that was marked Cave-in Club in scrawly handwriting above the biggest cave.

They walked up to the entrance. Looking inside, they could see the flickering light from the empty main room at the end of the passageway.

"The Cave-in Club don't look like it's doing much business," Georgie remarked.

"I don't think it ever was a real club, Georgie," Davy said. "Leastways not a club for decent folk."

"You mean this is Mason's hangout?"

"I bet it is." Davy began walking in.

Georgie had no choice but to follow him. The entryway was so small they had to crouch low.

"Yee-ouch!" Georgie cried as he hit his head.

"Duck," Davy said over his shoulder.

"Thanks for telling me," Georgie muttered. "This is almost as bad as crawling in a hollow log after a bear."

They crept along until they reached the main room. The fireplace's flames cast eerie, distorted shapes on the craggy walls. In the flickering orange light, all the shadows seemed to dance. Georgie shivered a little at the spookiness of it all.

He and Davy walked through the room, cautiously looking around. They saw the piles of rocks, crates, and barrels along the wall, but they didn't see the kegs hidden behind them.

Or the three men hidden behind the kegs.

Davy and Georgie silently spread out to cover different parts of the room, with their backs to each other. Georgie picked up a piece of wood from the ground and approached a barrel big enough for a person to hide in. With one hand he held the piece of wood over his head, ready to strike. With his other hand he cautiously pulled off the barrel's lid.

He had no idea what was happening behind him, and neither did Davy.

Slowly Big Harpe had crept out of his hiding place. His face was twisted into a fierce grimace. His fingers were tightened around the handle of his blade.

The razor-sharp steel glinted in the light. Big Harpe drew the blade back.

Aiming carefully, he took a swing at the back of Georgie's head.

CHAPTER 14

*hooosh!*

**W**hooosh! Just as the blade sliced through the air, Georgie bent down to look into the barrel. He felt only the breeze of Big Harpe's missed swing.

Big Harpe ducked back behind the powder keg, angry at having missed his target.

"Hmm," Georgie said, looking around. "Kinda drafty in here." He peered back into the barrel and saw that it was stuffed with Indian clothes. "Hey, Davy! Look what I found!"

Davy ran over. While he looked inside, Georgie spotted a tomahawk on the ground. He picked it up and examined the blade. "Lookee here. This is the same kind of fake we found sticking in that wrecked keelboat!"

Davy looked at the tomahawk, then lifted a Kaskaskia headdress out of the barrel. "This is the place where those varmints changed into Indians," Davy said.

"But where are they?" Georgie asked.

Davy was staring at the entrance to the back room. "Stay here," he said. "Maybe I can smoke something out."

As Davy disappeared into the shadowy darkness of the back room, Georgie felt a chill race up his spine. From the corner of his eye, he thought he saw a movement. He spun around.

There was nothing there, just flickering shadows.

He thought he saw something move again. Again, he whirled. And again. But each time he could only see the dancing shapes on the wall.

"Hey, Davy!" he called out nervously. "What's keeping you?"

"There's plenty of loot in here," Davy called back. "Come look at this stuff."

Georgie met him at the room's entrance. Davy had lit three torches that hung on the wall. Georgie whistled in awe at all the treasure chests and bags of money. "They wouldn't go off and leave all this," Georgie muttered. "Reckon they're still around here someplace. But where?"

Davy was already looking back into the main room. His eyes fixed on the thin, white powder trails that crisscrossed the floor like a big spider's web. He followed one of the trails to a small pile of rocks.

Shoving the rocks aside, he uncovered a powder keg.

He scanned the room. There were other piles of rocks, and piles of cases and barrels. When he spied a sudden movement behind a pile of crates to the left of him, a smile crossed his face. A powder trail led directly to that one.

If Davy were to light the trail, though, it would also explode the keg right next to him. So he reached down and swept away an opening in the powder so it would light only that one keg. Georgie handed him a torch.

"This ought to lead to something interesting," Davy said.

He lit the trail and quickly put the torch back. Smoke billowed upward as the flame raced along the powder path. Off to one side, a table began to twitch. Davy could see feet shifting beneath the long tablecloth. There was more movement on the other side of the room in a pile of crates.

Suddenly Mason bolted into the open.

*Kaboooooooooooooom!*

The exploding keg sent bits of wood and rubble flying. Davy and Georgie ducked. Mason tumbled head over heels, landing safely in the middle of the room.

As the smoke cleared, Little Harpe sprang out from under the table. Mason picked himself up off the floor, practically spitting with anger. Big Harpe emerged from his hiding place, this time clutching his hammer.

Mason was the first to attack. With a bloodcurdling cry, he hurled himself across the room at Davy.

He landed on the ground with a loud *whomp* as

Davy rolled away. Grabbing the piece of wood Georgie had used earlier, Davy jumped to his feet.

He saw Georgie rushing to help him, but both Harpe brothers were flying toward Georgie from opposite sides of the room.

"Look out!" Davy yelled.

Georgie ducked. Big Harpe swung his hammer. It sailed over Georgie's head—and bonked Little Harpe instead!

Little Harpe fell under the table. Furious, Big Harpe dropped the hammer, lifted an empty barrel, and threw it. It smashed into Georgie's stomach, sending him tumbling backward.

Big Harpe smiled. Now he could finish Georgie off. He started to lumber toward him.

Under the table, Little Harpe clutched the hammer that had bonked him. He spotted a pair of boots moving slowly inches from his nose. Thinking they belonged to Georgie, he drew his arm back and banged down hard.

"Yeeee-ouch!" Big Harpe hollered. "That was me, you idiot!"

Meanwhile, Davy and Mason were slugging it out. Mason staggered to the fireplace. He grabbed a red-hot poker and hurled it viciously at Davy.

Davy ducked out of the way, once again grabbing hold of the piece of wood. Mason yanked a chain off the floor.

The two of them circled each other. Mason swung the chain and Davy blocked it with the wood. The chain whipped around the wood, coiled like a spring.

With a strong flick of his wrist, Davy tossed the wood and chain across the room.

It almost hit Big Harpe, who stepped away in the nick of time. He found himself jammed into a corner. On the wall above his head, a torch blazed brightly. Big Harpe grabbed it and ran toward Georgie.

At the same time, Little Harpe came out from under the table, knocking it over right into Big Harpe's path.

"Yah-ungh!" Big Harpe grunted as his knees slammed into the table. The torch flew out of his hands. It arced through the air and fell to the ground right on top of some other powder trails!

*Tsshhhhhhh!* The powder sent sparks into the air as the flames raced toward several kegs at once. For a moment, Davy, Georgie, Mason, and the Harpe brothers all froze. They were all thinking the same thing. They had to get out of there. Fast!

Mason and the Harpes got to the passageway first. They scrambled through and ran outside.

Davy and Georgie weren't so lucky. They were only halfway through when the entire place blew up.

# CHAPTER 15

The ground shook. Davy and Georgie lost their balance. The passageway crumbled around them.

"Yeow, my head!" Georgie said.

Davy reached behind him and grabbed Georgie's arm. "Come on!" he shouted.

They got to their feet and stumbled toward the opening. A chunk of dirt and rock fell in front of them, blocking their way. Davy pushed it aside, coughing violently.

When the ground jolted again, Davy knew that the cave had collapsed behind them. It was only a matter of seconds before the passageway went, too.

With a final leap through the flying dirt, he plunged forward.

When Davy hit the ground, his eyes were covered with grit. But he noticed that the air smelled clear and fresh.

He was outside! He rubbed the dirt from his eyes

as best as he could. He opened them just in time to see the passageway crumble.

*"Georgie!"* He raced back toward the cave.

But a nearby voice made him stop short. "Easy, partner. I think that club is closed."

Davy spun around. Georgie was sprawled on the ground right next to where Davy had been. He was sooty-faced but alive.

Next to Georgie were Mason, Little Harpe, and Big Harpe—safely in the clutches of Big Mike and his men!

"Finally found you varmints!" Mike said to Davy. "Thought you'd give us the slip, eh?"

Mason and his men scowled. Their days as Kaskaskias were over. And the Ohio was safe for travelers once again.


Well, legend has it that the *Gullywhumper* made it back to the Chickasaw camp on the very night of the full moon. Black Eagle sent a messenger to the Kaskaskias, and the two tribes had a ceremony for Davy, Georgie, and Mike like no one had ever seen before.

They say the celebration lasted four days and four nights. No one knows exactly what happened there. Nothing was ever written down, and everyone who was there kept it a secret.

All anyone knows is that it was the most beautiful four days of weather up and down the Ohio and the Mississippi. Then again, maybe that's all anyone needed to know.

# EPILOG

Davy Crockett is perhaps the most famous folk hero of the American frontier. He was born in 1786 and grew up in the rugged country of eastern Tennessee, where his father ran a small country inn. Business was never very good, and the family often relied on young Davy's hunting skills to put food on the table. But even in tough times, Davy had a knack for amusing himself and others with tall tales, a skill that was to later become part of the Crockett legend.

In 1806, Davy married Polly Finley, and they began to raise a family. As the frontier grew more crowded with settlers, Davy and Polly kept moving their family farther west. In 1813, Davy and his family moved for the last time, deep into western Tennessee.

Davy championed the rights of Native Americans in an era marked by great injustice toward Indian people. In 1813, he joined the army in an effort to negotiate an end to the Creek War. His efforts were successful, and in the process he earned the respect of both sides.

Davy returned from the war a hero and was so popular that

*he was eventually elected to the United States Congress, where he served three terms. During that time, he helped draft a treaty that would have enabled the Indian people to keep their land. But in 1835, when Congress decided to break the treaty, and his efforts to save it failed, he decided not to run for reelection.*

*In 1836, Davy Crockett, along with his trusted companion Georgie Russel, joined a small band of brave American settlers under siege at the Alamo in San Antonio, Texas, which was then part of Mexico. The settlers fought long and valiantly in the name of freedom to defend themselves against the Mexican Army, but in the end their numbers were no match for the huge force amassed against them. The enemy soldiers finally overran the Alamo, killing every man, woman, and child within its walls. Davy Crockett died as he had lived—an American hero. And the phrase "Remember the Alamo!" lived on to inspire and unite the Americans in Texas, who eventually won their freedom from Mexico and brought Texas into the United States.*